Jack
and the
Beanstalk

DK | Penguin
Random
House

Illustration Giuseppe Di Lernia
Written and retold by Melanie Joyce
Project editor Clare Lloyd
Design assistant Eleanor Bates
Jacket designer Charlotte Jennings
Jacket co-ordinator Issy Walsh
Producer John Casey
Pre-production producer Heather Blagden
Managing editor Penny Smith
Managing art editor Mabel Chan
Creative director Helen Senior
Publishing director Sarah Larter

First published in Great Britain in 2019 by
Dorling Kindersley Limited
One Embassy Gardens, 8 Viaduct Gardens,
London, SW11 7BW

A CIP catalogue record for this book
is available from the British Library.
ISBN: 978-0-2413-7099-5

Printed and bound in China

For the curious
www.dk.com

MIX
Paper from
responsible sources
FSC™ C018179

This book was made with Forest
Stewardship Council™ certified paper –
one small step in DK's commitment to a
sustainable future. For more information
go to www.dk.com/our-green-pledge

Notes for Parents and Carers

Here are some ideas for discussing important themes in *Jack and the Beanstalk* with young children. Use these notes to prompt discussion during and after reading the book.

- Why is Jack's mother upset with him at the beginning of the story? If you had a cow, would you sell it for some magic beans? Talk about what might happen if a beanstalk grew in your garden.

- Why do you think Jack keeps climbing the beanstalk? Can you name the three things that Jack takes from the giant? Do you think the giant is friendly?

- Why does the giant chase Jack? Do you think that if Jack had asked nicely, the giant would have given him some gold? Discuss the importance of asking for things in the right way.

Once upon a time, a boy called Jack lived with his mother in a little cottage. They were very poor and only had the milk from their cow to drink.

One day, the cow stopped giving milk.
"We need money for food," said Jack's mother.
"Take our cow to market and sell her."

Jack set off to market. On the way, he met an old man who wanted to buy the cow.

"I'll pay you with these magic beans,"
said the man. "They will grow up to the sky."
"Okay," said Jack. He took the beans and gave
his cow to the man.

When Jack's mother found out what he had done, she was very upset. "You sold our cow for a handful of beans?" she cried, flinging them out of the window.

That night Jack fell asleep feeling very unhappy. Outside, rain fell on the enchanted beans.

The next morning, Jack saw that an enormous beanstalk had grown where the beans had fallen!

Jack dashed outside. The towering beanstalk stretched up through the clouds. "Where does it go?" he wondered.

Without giving it a second thought, Jack started to climb the beanstalk! He climbed higher and higher until the cottage was far below.

Above the clouds, Jack found a gigantic castle. He tiptoed into the dining room. "I wonder who lives here?" he whispered.

There, on a huge table, was
a big bag of shiny gold coins.

Suddenly the ground began to shake. Jack heard heavy
footsteps. Thump! Thump! Thump! Jack ran and hid.

An enormous giant appeared.
He twitched his nose and sniffed.

"Fee-fi-fo-fum, I smell the blood
of an Englishman. Be he alive,
or be he dead, I'll grind his
bones to make my bread!"

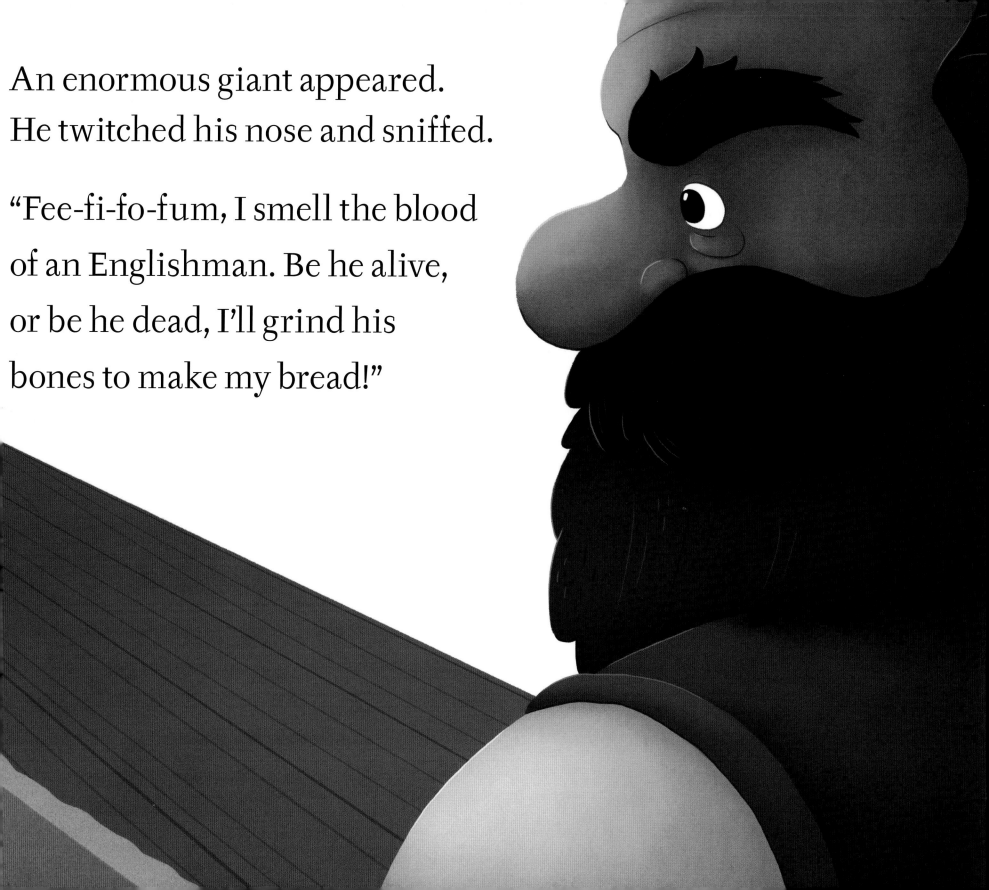

The giant looked around, but he couldn't see Jack. He sat down and gobbled up his food. Soon he fell fast asleep.

Jack crept out from his hiding place. He grabbed the big bag of gold coins and ran. Before long he was climbing back down the beanstalk.

Jack and his mother were
rich. But they spent too much
and soon the gold coins ran
out. So Jack climbed back up
the beanstalk to the castle.

"Fee-fi-fo-fum, I smell the blood of an Englishman,"
said the giant as he stroked a hen that laid eggs of gold.

Just as before, the giant could not find Jack, so he gobbled up his food and fell asleep. Jack grabbed the hen and climbed back down the beanstalk.

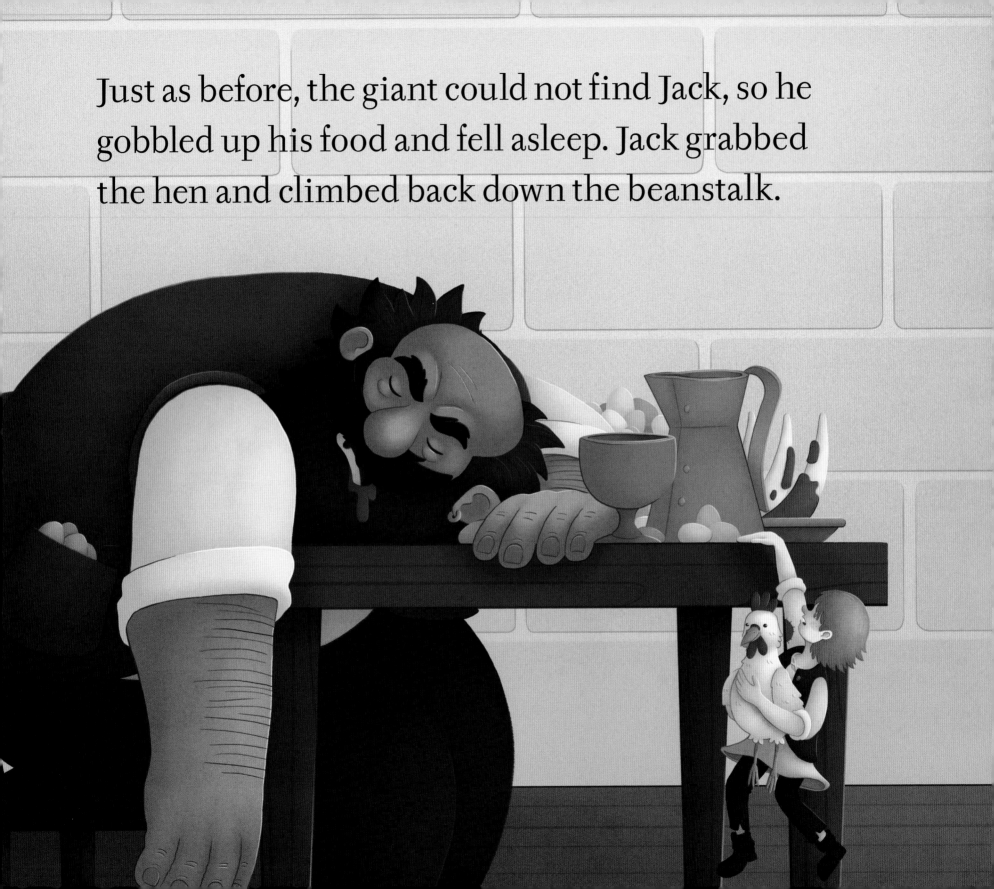

The gold eggs made Jack and his mother rich
again. But Jack wanted more. He climbed back
up the beanstalk to the castle.

Jack found the giant dozing, while a golden harp played sweet music. "Fee-fi-fo-fum," muttered the giant in his sleep.

Jack snatched the golden harp, but it shrieked,
"Master! Master!" The giant leapt up. He chased
Jack all the way to the beanstalk.

"FEE-FI-FO-FUM!"
roared the angry giant,
as he climbed down the
beanstalk after Jack.

"Mother, fetch an axe!" shouted
Jack when he reached the ground.
With a chop-chop-chop, he cut
the beanstalk down.

It fell with a terrible crash, and that was the end of the angry giant.

Jack and his mother kept the hen that laid gold eggs, and the golden harp that played sweet music. They lived happily ever after and never saw the angry giant again.